Tuesdays with Henry

MAKING MOMENTS WITH GRANDMA ELLEN

WRITTEN BY MARLANE PENTELECHUK
ILLUSTRATED BY LYN VIK

FriesenPress

Suite 300 - 990 Fort St
Victoria, BC, V8V 3K2
Canada

www.friesenpress.com

Copyright © 2019 by Marlane Pentelechuk
First Edition — 2019

ISBN
978-1-5255-4459-0 (Hardcover)
978-1-5255-4460-6 (Paperback)
978-1-5255-4461-3 (eBook)

1. Juvenile Fiction

Distributed to the trade by The Ingram Book Company

DEDICATION

For Grandma Ellen and Henry
"Every moment is a gift!"
~Marlane

For Dad
"Love leaves a memory that cannot be lost."
~Lyn

It is Tuesday. That means "Gram Day" for Henry so that Momma can get a little work done. Gram and Henry get a few things done too!

Some Tuesdays they go to the park or work in the yard. Some Tuesdays they visit Pop on the field to take him some lunch and ride in his big, red tractor. But MOST Tuesdays they go to visit Grandma Ellen, who lives in a tall orange building with some other grandmas and a few grandpas too.

Grandma Ellen is really Henry's "great-grandma", but he just calls her "Grandma".

Grandma Ellen calls Henry "Little One" because she forgets his name. She forgets a lot of other things too, and she doesn't have many memories left. Gram says that Grandma Ellen is losing her memories, but she loves the moments. MEMORIES are things that happened in the past, but MOMENTS are things that are happening right now, so we try to make every moment count.

Sometimes Grandma Ellen forgets who Gram is, even though Gram is her daughter, but Gram says, "That's okay, Henry. WE know who SHE is, don't we? That's all that matters."

It's a warm, sunny day, and the park next to Grandma Ellen's building looks really inviting. But first things first ... time to make some moments with Grandma Ellen! They head to the front door and sign their names at the desk. Henry takes the special "magic" key and waves it across the red light next to the door to Grandma Ellen's unit.

"OPEN SESAME!" they giggle. The red light turns green, and the door opens for them.

Without the magic key, the door stays locked. Henry wonders if this is like a jail for forgetful people. "Is Grandma Ellen being punished?" he asks.

Gram says, "No, Henry. The lock on the door is to keep Grandma Ellen out of harm's way. Sometimes, people who forget, like Grandma Ellen, might not think to dress properly for the weather. They might forget where they are going or how to get back on their own. They could get lost or hurt or worse. But Grandma Ellen can come out with us anytime she wants. We can take her out for coffee, or a walk in the park, or even shopping to the mall, and then we bring her right back here where she is safe and sound. Every outing is a new moment for Grandma Ellen to enjoy!"

Henry is HAPPY for the lock and the magic key so that Grandma Ellen stays protected when he's not around to help her put on her coat or hold her hand in the parking lot.

Inside Grandma Ellen's unit, the first person they see is Amy. Amy is Grandma Ellen's "person". She makes sure Grandma Ellen is okay all day. She helps her shower and brushes her teeth. She helps Grandma Ellen get dressed and put on her red lipstick. She makes sure Grandma Ellen takes her medicine at the right time and watches out for her all day long.

Gram says, "Amy is an angel!"

There are other "angels" on Grandma Ellen's unit too. They are kind and patient and so loving to all the grandmas and grandpas. Gram says that the angels work really hard! Henry wonders where the angels hide their wings.

Gram says, "REAL wings would probably get in the way of all the work they have to do. These wings are INVISIBLE!"

Henry imagines big, beautiful wings on Amy's back, and it makes him smile.

Amy takes Henry to the kitchen for a cookie, and then Henry gets to work making a few moments count. First, he goes to give Grandma Ellen a big hug. She loves it! Grandma Ellen is so happy to see Henry and Gram, even though she isn't quite sure who they are. She KNOWS she knows them, but she can't quite figure out HOW she knows them.

That's okay ... Henry and Gram know!

The "HELLO" and the "HUG" make a moment, and Grandma Ellen is in it!

Henry then makes his rounds visiting with all the other grandmas and grandpas.

Gram says that not many "littles" come to visit this place. "Henry, you are a BIG ATTRACTION!"

Henry makes sure he shakes hands or hugs whoever wants to visit with him. The grandmas and grandpas get pretty excited. Henry has a name for each one of them … Baba, who always speaks Ukrainian; Bella, who always speaks Italian; and Mama, who is Ethiopian. Mr. Sing loves to hum and whistle for Henry, and Mr. Will likes to talk about Henry's toy cars. The Grandma D's—Daisy and Doreen—don't really go for hugs, but they pat him on the head and give him warm smiles. Henry makes a moment with all of them.

Some of the grandmas who try to talk to Henry are really hard to understand. Gram says that sometimes their words just come out wrong and don't make any sense. It's important not to ask too many questions or to be disrespectful. He watches how Gram just nods and listens. She laughs when THEY laugh, and she looks serious when THEY look serious. He tries to do the same, but it's kind of hard. Most of the time, Henry leaves those moments for Gram to handle.

Henry wonders why some grandmas and grandpas don't speak at all.

Gram says, "Sometimes they just forget the words for things, and then it gets harder and harder to speak at all—but that doesn't mean they don't listen."

So Henry goes over to say hello to the quiet grandmas and grandpas, so that they can listen to his visit and have a little moment too.

Sometimes the grandmas and grandpas get sad or angry. One time, one of the grandmas was VERY upset when Henry came to visit. She was crying and shaking her cane. Henry was a little scared.

Gram said, "Henry, the grandmas are real people with real feelings. They get sad or frustrated or lonely or tired or angry just like we do."

Henry didn't know what to do. But the angels knew. The angels were tender and patient with that grandma. They talked to her quietly and calmly and then took her gently by the hand to her room. That grandma had a little rest and then she was much better.

Gram says, "Sometimes moments can be tough, but they are just moments and not memories—and that can be a blessing!"

Henry understands. He always feels much better after a nap, and he certainly has had a few "moments" that he would rather forget too!

Today, Henry and Gram bring Grandma Ellen a special coffee and a muffin. They go outside to the courtyard to have a little picnic. They chat about the weather and about the coffee and about Gram's new outfit, which isn't really that new.

Gram says, "It's important to include Grandma Ellen in the conversation so she doesn't feel left out." Talking about stuff she has to remember is really hard, so they stick to the stuff that's right before her eyes. Or they tell her what they've been doing or what they're going to be doing. She loves to hear about all of it, even though she forgets pretty fast. They just tell her again … and again. It's not hard to repeat it, and Henry and Gram love to see Grandma Ellen's face light up again … and again … and AGAIN! The MOMENTS are MULTIPLYING!

Pretty soon, Ned comes around. He is like a really big kid who loves to play games and organize activities for the grandmas and grandpas. Ned makes sure that all the holidays are celebrated here too, like Christmas and Easter and even Remembrance Day. Most of the grandmas and grandpas don't really KNOW when a special holiday is coming up because they FORGET, but Ned and his crew make the moments count. They have special food and music and party favors. Sometimes the grandmas and grandpas sing and dance. It's pretty fun for Henry and Gram to watch those moments!

Gram was really sad that Grandma Ellen wasn't able to come to family Christmas at Gram and Pop's house this year. Henry was a little sad too.

Gram explained, "It's just too hard on Grandma Ellen to remember everyone's name and to try to think of all the words to say. She gets really quiet and acts a little scared and not like Grandma Ellen at all! Even though we want her at OUR place, it's really best that she stays here at HER place!"

So the whole family came and brought some Christmas moments to her. They brought little treat bags for all the grandmas and grandpas and gave them all Christmas hugs and handshakes, and then they let them have their lunch. Henry knows they won't remember that Christmas moment, but it's an awesome memory for him!

Sometimes when they visit, Henry and Gram join the activities, but mostly Grandma Ellen goes on her own to play games or listen to music or go to chapel. The chapel is really cool. Sometimes Henry and Gram go there to pray a prayer for Grandma Ellen and the other grandmas and grandpas and for the angels too. Grandma Ellen loves to go to the chapel times to pray and to sing the old hymns. Funny, Grandma Ellen forgets so many things, but she NEVER forgets how to pray or worship.

Gram says, "Well, Henry, the brain might forget, but the HEART ALWAYS REMEMBERS. God is all about the heart ... so I guess it's a special 'God moment' for Grandma Ellen."

Henry likes that God has moments with Grandma Ellen too.

Very soon the time comes for Henry and Gram to say their goodbyes to Grandma Ellen, the angels, and to all the grandmas and grandpas. Some have already forgotten that they were there and act surprised and happy to see Henry again. It's like TWO visits in one!

Everyone waves goodbye, and Henry promises to come back again next Tuesday!

Out comes the magic key, and off they go to play in the park outside the tall orange building. They made some great moments for Grandma Ellen today—and a few good memories for Henry. Gram says that even though Grandma Ellen may not have any memories of this visit, she just might remember how these moments made her FEEL, and they made her feel AWESOME today. This makes Henry feel awesome!

Then Gram says "Henry, you know Grandma Ellen probably WON'T remember that you promised to come next Tuesday."

Henry just smiles. "I know ... Grandma Ellen lives in the moments. SHE will probably forget, but WE will remember, and that's all that matters!"

FOR PARENTS:

Visiting your loved ones with dementia is so important! Those struggling with the disease can often feel lonely and isolated. Patients, even in the later stages of dementia, can benefit from visits from young children who often connect at a deep emotional level. Preparation is a key element to ensuring that a visit is successful. Here are some things to keep in mind:

1. Check with the facility to pick a good time to visit to avoid conflicting with daily routines and schedules. Respect meal, nap, or organized event times. Gram and Henry are careful not to interfere with Grandma Ellen's daily routine and are not offended when she wants to go for a nap or head to the games room when they come to visit. They keep visit times short and sweet but try to come regularly.

2. Talk about the visit ahead of time with your child. Gram talks to Henry a lot about Grandma Ellen. It helps Henry to understand that Grandma Ellen is still "Grandma", but that she has a few challenges that we can accept and work around. Fear and anxiety are lessened by keeping it simple.

3. Focus on being gentle and respectful so that residents and staff are not upset by the visit. Henry and Gram are careful to respect everyone's personal space. They don't hug everyone, but they do try to include and acknowledge everyone who interacts with them in a polite manner. Henry doesn't run down the halls or use his "outside voice" when visiting the unit.

4. Bringing a toy or book to share can be a great conversation starter. Dementia patients live in the moment, so concentrating on what is in front of them works really well to facilitate interaction. The grandmas and grandpas often roll Henry's toy car back and forth with him or enjoy looking at a picture book with him. No pressure to remember or think about a topic makes the visit less awkward too.

5. Sometimes the odd behaviour of some dementia patients can be confusing for children. Depending on the situation, simple explanations, distraction or even a quick exit might be the answers. Keeping calm is the key to alleviating fear or anxiety in children. Staff members are generally well trained and quick to deal with unacceptable behaviour should it occur.

6. Visiting your loved one with dementia fills an important emotional need in the patient, but it also creates beautiful and profound memories for your child. Henry learns many valuable lessons about service to others, about respect for the elderly, and about the power of love and empathy for those who are lost, lonely, or sick.

ACKNOWLEDGEMENTS

Many thanks and much love to the many family members, friends, and colleagues, who took the time to read, consult, pray, and champion this special project. Special thanks to ...

Amira, Ellen's "angel", for the inspiration and the challenge.

Lyn, for the beautiful illustrations and for putting
up with all my quirky demands.

Mark, my brother and publishing "Sherpa".

Erin, my daughter, my designer, and my mental twin.

Nick, Janelle, Matthew and Jack, my family and my cheerleaders.

Darren, my husband, my one and only.

Henry, my first grandson, for all the Tuesdays and all the moments.

Emil, my dad, who would have loved reading this story aloud.

Ellen, my mom, who is still my mom. Even if she forgets, I remember!

ABOUT THE AUTHOR

A former elementary school teacher, Marlane Pentelechuk retired from the classroom to care for her aging parents. When her mother was placed in a secure care facility due to her advanced dementia, Marlane learned many lessons about interacting with Alzheimer's and dementia patients and how appreciated and significant regular visits can be, not only for the patient but also for the visitor.

Now "Gram" to little Henry, she finds great delight in having him join her as they make moments together for Grandma Ellen and the other residents on the unit. Her desire is that this story would inspire other families with loved ones who have dementia to find value in regular visits and look for ways to make them meaningful, if only for the "moment".

Marlane Pentelechuk lives in Sherwood Park, Alberta, Canada with her husband, Darren.

ABOUT THE ILLUSTRATOR – LYN VIK

Tuesdays with Henry is the first book illustration for Lyn Vik, a nature and wildlife artist from Leduc County, Alberta, Canada.

She was honored to have been given the opportunity to help create such a wonderfully written and touching tribute to the many who struggle with Alzheimer's and dementia, and to their families who love them.

Lyn hopes readers will find as much enjoyment getting to know Henry and Grandma Ellen as she did illustrating them.

9 781525 544606